# CHRIS HEATH FARM

# GREG SEELEY

A poignant, heartfelt story with a keen sensitivity to family. Greg reminds us that our loved ones who have passed on are forever only a whisper away.

Pamela Allegretto, Author "Bridge of Sighs and Dreams"

Katherine Jean Howell is a retired and recently widowed physician living in a Chicago high-rise. Just weeks before Christmas, she receives a disturbing e-mail. Her cousin who owns the family farm back in Iowa is planning to tear down the old homestead to make more crop space. What happens next, you won't believe. I promise "Christmas at the Heath Farm" will both warm your heart and bring a tear to your eye. It did to mine when I was writing it.

CHRISTMAS AT THE HEATH FARM

Printed in the United States of America

First Printing, November 2019

ISBN 978-1-69079441-7

 Edited by Katie-bree Reeves of Fair Crack of the Whip Proofreading and Editing

Cover design by Paul Copello of Designistrate.com

Cover art by Greg Seeley

This a work of fiction. Names, characters, places, and incidents are either products of the author's imagination Any resemblance to actual persons, living or dead, is coincidental.

# OTHER BOOKS BY GREG SEELEY

## *THE HORSE LAWYER AND OTHER POEMS*

## *TRACTOR BONES AND RUSTED TRUCKS: TALES AND RECOLLECTIONS OF A HEARTLAND BABY BOOMER*

## *HENRY'S PRIDE: A NOVEL OF THE CIVIL WAR*

## *HENRY'S LAND; A BROKEN PEACE*

## *HENRY'S PROMISE: RECKONINGS*
## *(COMING 2020)*

## All titles available at Amazon.com

# DEDICATION

This story is lovingly dedicated to my parents and my grandparents as well as to my wife's parents and their parents who lived through the Great Depression. These hardy souls experienced first-hand the struggles, privations, and sacrifices that came with farm life during that difficult time. Supported by community, faith, and family, they emerged from this great trial even stronger than before and passed these same values on to those of us who followed. To these generations of our family thank you.

# ACKNOWLEDGEMENTS

A special thank you to all of the friends, relatives, and colleagues who have contributed their time, support, effort, and talent to this endeavor.

Thank you to my editor, Katie-bree Reeves, whose amazing sense of phrasing and style have once again helped turn a raw manuscript into a finished project worthy of readers' time and attention. To my cover designer, Paul Copello, for his care in creating a design depicting the real essence of my story. To my author friends Steven Malone, and J.D.R. Hawkins whose critiques and plot suggestions helped bring my characters to life and give them depth.

Most of all, thank you to my wife Carolyn - for your love, support, patience, and understanding as I continue to indulge my passion of writing historical stories and novels.

# CAST OF CHARCTERS

### Part I – A Heath Family Christmas

Harry and Mildred Heath – an impoverished Iowa farm couple during the Great Depression

Phillip Heath – their son

Lilly Heath – their daughter

George Albers – an amazing man who shows up unexpectedly at the Heath farm

Katherine Jean Howell - Lilly's daughter and only child

Jerry Heath – Phillip's son,  Lilly's cousin


### Part II – A Heath Family Christmas Reunion

Katherine Jean Howell-Adams – A retired pediatrician

Keith Adams – Katherine's second husband

Jerry Heath – Phillip's son, Katherine's cousin

Janice Heath – Jerry's wife

Alan Heath – Jerry and Janice' son

Theresa Heath – Alan's wife

Elaine Heath – Alan and Thera's daughter

Tommy Heath – Alan and Theresa's son

# PART I:

# A HEATH FAMILY
# CHRISTMAS

GERTRUDE
AND
GRETCHEN
Lilly HEATH

# CHAPTER I

Katherine Jean Howell, recent widow and retired pediatrician, stood at the window of her thirty-second-floor condominium and stared at Lake Michigan. Well, not really at it, towards it. On a clear spring or summer day, she could have scanned the conglomeration of sailboats, motor yachts, and freighters. But this was mid-December in Chicago. All she could make out as dusk approached were the faint city lights in the distance trying bravely to shine through the increasingly heavy snowfall.

The day had started brightly enough, hardly a cloud in sight. By noon, the sun had already begun to disappear behind thickening, black clouds. Now, at four o'clock, she could see less than the length of a football field. Soon, it would not be more than a few feet. She felt for the commuters fighting their way home on this Thursday. What she did not miss at all were the daily trips to and from her office in such weather over the last thirty-five plus years. She missed her nurses and her staff. She missed her colleagues at the clinic. Most of all, she missed the children. But driving through freezing rain, snow, ice, and slush to and from work? No, she didn't miss that at all.

She had lost track of the time spent mesmerized by the wisps of snowflakes being buffeted about by the wind. She recalled the still half-full mug of coffee being pleasingly hot when she left the couch and laptop. Now it was room temperature. With a sigh, she dumped it in the sink and inserted a refill in the Keurig. Fresh coffee in hand, she returned to the couch and the email she had received earlier this afternoon from her cousin, Jerry.

"How could he do this?" she muttered out loud. Two weeks before Christmas, her first one without David, and now this. Wasn't it hard enough already? Sadness and anger wrestled each other for control of her brain – back and forth, not really opposing each other, but at odds just enough to give her a headache. She took a sip of the coffee and contemplated whether to reply. She didn't really know what to say. It was his property. He had the right to do with it as he wished, but now? At Christmas? And this Christmas, especially?

*Dear Kate,*

*Janice and I are hoping that you will change your mind and join us here in Florida over Christmas. We would love to have you.*

"So far so good."

*There is something else you need to know. Since Alan has taken over farming the place, I am pretty much leaving the decision making to him. Grandpa and Grandma Heath's house continues to deteriorate and we think it best to go ahead and tear it down. Alan says the rows of trees along the lane need to come out, too. It would create more crop space since he can barely get the planter and the combine between them to reach the field as it is. We will not be back to Iowa before planting time and he wants to go ahead and do it in time for the spring plowing. The barn and other outbuildings are in better shape so he plans to keep them for storage.*

*Love,*

*Jerry.*

Slamming the laptop's cover down harder than she meant to, she picked up the remote and turned on the television. She spent the remainder of the evening snacking and binging on old episodes of *Friends*. It required little thought. Each episode was pretty much the same as the one before - mind-numbing - just what she needed right now.

Finally, she crawled into bed, buried her face in the pillow, pulled the covers up over her head, and sobbed herself to sleep. "Oh, David, I miss you so much!"

Sometime later, she didn't know when, she found herself standing at the window. Odd, she didn't remember getting out of bed. The snow had stopped falling but there were no city lights to be seen through the dim gray light– only bright stars shining over a distant and bare tree line. The moon was nearly full and it reflected now over a field of drifted, undisturbed snow. And the curtains didn't feel right. She hadn't had willowy, lace curtains for years. She touched the window. It had divided panes and was cold, icy cold and frosted, so unlike the thermal windows of her condo that were warm even on the coldest Chicago days and nights.

And the room was cold – a shivering, goose bump-inducing kind of cold. She headed for the closet to fetch a warm fleece robe. "Where's the closet? Where's the light switch?"

The moonlight revealed a robe draped over the back of a chair. "I didn't leave that there," she wondered. "Where did that chair come from?"

She must be dreaming. She had to be. But everything seemed so real? She walked toward where the bathroom should be but found that it wasn't.

"This is all wrong. I need to call someone. Where is my cell phone? Why isn't it on the night table where I left it? I always leave it there"

She remembered being cold and returned to the chair to retrieve the robe. "This isn't my robe. Why is it so wooly and scratchy? Why is it so small?" She curled up in the chair, pulled the robe over herself like a shawl, and covered her eyes with her hands. "I'm just exhausted. That has to be it. I'll will be fine in the morning."

Suddenly, a voice broke the silence, echoing into the room. She hadn't heard that voice in years but it had always given her comfort and soothed away any childhood tears. "Lilly, it's time to get up. You need to get ready for school!"

The voice seemed to come from downstairs. But the condo didn't have a downstairs – only sound-proof floors below.

Grandma Mildred?!

"Coming Mama! A small voice answered"

The voice came from the bed, interrupting Katherine's thoughts and surprising her further.

"Mama?"

Lilly rolled back the thick layers of covers and sat up. It was still dark out although a hint of daylight was beginning to shine through the room's only window. The girl crawled from bed and lit the kerosene lamp on the dresser.

Suddenly, everything in the room looked familiar to Katherine– the dresser, the bed with its ornately carved headboard and footboard, the little bookcase in the corner, and the shelf of dolls near the door to the hall. She had seen it many times when visiting Grandma and Grandpa. She had slept in that very bed. She had kept her clothes in the very same dresser. She had played with those exact same dolls. She had sat in this same chair and read her favorite Nancy Drew mysteries. "Mama?" she whispered in awe.

Mama looked exactly like the pictures in the album Katherine remembered so well from her childhood and now kept safely tucked away on the top shelf of her closet in the condo. "Mama?" she whispered again. "You can't hear or see me, can you? Of course, you can't. I'm not born yet!"

Lilly walked to the chair where Katherine had curled up. The robe was draped over the back of the chair once more, exactly as she had left it before crawling into bed. It fit the little girl perfectly. In awe, Katherine reached out to hug her but was disappointed when her arms found only air. Sadly, she realized that any attempts to talk to Grandma Mildred or Grandpa Harry or to hug them would also be futile.

"Lilly, are you up!"

"Yes, Mama!" Lilly stood at the dresser mirror, barely tall enough to see herself in it, as more daylight began to filter into the room. Picking up a brush, she ran it through her bright red hair. It reminded Katherine of her own hair that had long-since lost its youthful luster.

"You need to hurry. Your breakfast will get cold."

The homey smell of bacon and eggs and fresh hot coffee wafted up the stairs and into Katherine's nose.

"Your brother is already down here. Your daddy will be in from the barn soon."

"Phillip. Oh, Uncle Phillip. I miss you," Katherine sighed. It seemed impossible that he had now been gone for fourteen years

Lilly sat in the chair beside Katherine and pulled up the leggings that would keep her warm as she walked to school. There would easily have been room for both of them in the big, overstuffed chair. Lilly was so tiny. But, of course, it didn't matter.

"Which of us isn't really here?" Katherine asked Lilly, perplexed, aware her question would remain unanswered. She watched as her mother pulled on her wool dress and buttoned it up the back.

Shortly after, Lilly finished putting on her shoes and blew out the lamp. The room was awash with daylight now but Katherine again found herself cold without the robe. She debated whether to crawl into that comforting bed or to follow Mama downstairs. The bacon, eggs and coffee smelled enticing but she knew that none of them were for her. At least she would have a chance to see Grandma Mildred and Grandpa Harry as she had only seen them in the photo album – young, hair not yet gray, walking straight and easily. She could see Uncle Phillip again and, for the first time, as a young boy. She eyed the bed and doorway cautiously. Not since she was a child, had she gone into anyone else's kitchen dressed only in her pajamas. But, then again, this wasn't someone else's kitchen. It was Grandma Mildred's kitchen. Besides, no one would see her. She gave the bed a longing glance then headed for the door, and silently followed Lilly down the stairs.

Katherine didn't recall changing out of her pajamas but as she reached the bottom of the stairway, she found herself wearing an outfit of jeans, a red and white sweater, and the high-top brown boots she had purchased only yesterday at Macy's. Mama had closed the stairway door behind her to keep the warm air of the kitchen from being 'wasted' upstairs.

Grandma Mildred's kitchen wasn't at all what Katherine remembered from her childhood. The familiar white electric range was gone. In its place sat a large, black cast iron wood-burning range. Also gone was the kitchen sink. By the window was a sturdy pine table covered with a blue and white gingham oilcloth. On the table sat a large white enamel dishpan next to a matching water bucket and dipper.

Where she remembered the Frigidaire, an oak icebox with several small doors and one large one stood in its place. Grandma's blue Formica-top kitchen table, along with its matching chrome and vinyl chairs, were nowhere to be found. Instead, in the middle of the kitchen, sat a large, round, oak pedestal table and matching chairs with cane seats.

There were neither a kitchen counter nor cupboards. Shelves along one wall held most of the cups, saucers, plates and bowls while another set of shelves on the floor underneath contained pots, pans, and skillets. Nearby was what Katherine had seen advertised in antique shops as a Hoosier cabinet. It consisted of an upper section with doors, behind which were kept salt, pepper, sugar, coffee and baking soda. Underneath was a tambour that rolled up to reveal more storage and a pullout enamel work surface for rolling out pie crusts and cutting up chickens. There was also a built-in flour bin and sifter. At the bottom, there were more doors and a metal-lined drawer for keeping bread away from the mice and bugs.

On the wall next to the door that led to the wash-up room, hung a calendar featuring a picture of some brightly colored roosters. Katherine stared at the date for a moment, allowing it all to sink in. '**DECEMBER 1935**'

"Mama, you are only seven!" she exclaimed.

Absorbed in the changes to the kitchen Katherine, had not, at first, lent her attention to its occupants. Upon hearing voices, she snapped her eyes to the dinner table. Here they were. Here was Grandpa Harry, in his faded, patched-up, Key-Imperial overalls sitting at the table, reading the *Des Moines Register*. Not yet an aging farmer with thinning white hair and an equally white, drooping mustache, he was young and fit, clean-shaven, with dark brown hair that showed just a small touch of gray around the temples. His hands were smooth and un-callused, yet to show the toll of many more years to come working in the fields and tending livestock. Here was Grandma Mildred, too, her beautiful red hair, cut in a bob that was the new style of the day. She wore a faded house dress covered by an apron made from a cloth sack that had once contained laying mash for the chickens. The beginning-to-wrinkle skin Katherine remembered from her childhood appeared only creamy and soft.

Uncle Phillip walked in from the wash-up room with a fresh bucket of water. He stood with his back to the kitchen as he filled the hot water reservoir at the end of the range. "Uncle Phillip!" Katherine exclaimed as he turned around, knowing he wouldn't hear her. "What a handsome young man you are!"

Harry folded his paper and laid it aside as Mildred set a plate of bacon and eggs on the table in front of him. "I found the perfect Christmas tree," he announced. "It's down by the creek near the gate to the timber."

Lilly clapped her hands gleefully. "When can we go get it?" she excitedly asked. "I'm so anxious for Christmas!"

"Not yet, Sugar. Christmas is still too far away. If we bring it in now, half the needles will fall off before Santa Claus sees it. You want it to be green and pretty for Santa, don't you?"

"Of course, I do, Daddy."

Katherine longed for her own childhood innocence – Santa Claus, the Tooth Fairy, and the Easter Bunny. She and David had never been able to have a child of their own. She regretted that they had never adopted, especially now, with David gone. She had seen so many babies and children pass through her practice whom she would have taken home with her in a heartbeat – particularly ones who appeared neglected or with special needs - ones whose parents seemed to have considered them a burden rather than a gift. But with her practice and David's constant travel for his construction business, they had just never gotten around to it. But, enough of that! That time had long-since passed her by. It was gone.

"I can hardly wait for lunch," Lilly announced.

"Oh Land, Lilly!" Grandma Mildred chimed in as she set down a bowl of hot oatmeal before the child. "You haven't even had your breakfast yet."

"It's not that, Mama." While we eat our lunch, Miss Ellen always reads to us. She's going to start another book today. She says it's brand new. It's called *National Velvet* and she says it's going to be about a little girl and her horse. When can I have a pony, Daddy?"

Before Grandpa could answer, Phillip chimed in, "I liked *The Call of the Wild* better. It has adventure. I wish she would just read that to us again."

"Silly," Lilly retorted. "How can you know if you like it better when she hasn't read this one to us yet?"

"I know *The Call of the Wild* isn't about girls!"

"That's enough, children," Grandma rebuked them both. Grandpa Harry tried his best to hide his grin but was caught winking at both of them. "I declare, Papa. You're as bad as they are! Now, all three of you, be quiet and eat your breakfast before it gets cold. Lord, what's a woman to do?"

# CHAPTER II

As it always does that time of year, nighttime came early.
By mid-afternoon, ominous gray clouds had already
blocked out most of the sunlight. By early evening, it was
snowing. Katherine couldn't tell how hard the snow was
coming down or from which direction the wind was
blowing. Unlike flakes in the city, silhouetted against the
streetlights, here they became invisible, consumed by the
complete darkness outside.

Unseen, she looked out the kitchen window but saw only
her own reflection mirrored against the golden glow of
kerosene lamps. Behind her, the family went about their
business – Grandma and Mama clearing away supper
dishes, Grandpa settling into a chair by the stove, lighting
that ever-present pipe, and Phillip poring over his new issue
of *Popular Mechanics*. She remembered Uncle Phillip
telling her of his childhood dream of becoming an aviator
and how he idolized Charles Lindbergh. Perhaps, he was
reading an article about airplanes.

Grandpa's face was hidden behind the pages of the *Des
Moines Register*. Smoke arose from behind the paper and
curled its way toward the ceiling. Eventually, he folded the
paper and placed it in his lap. He took the pipe from his
mouth just long enough to speak. "Gall darned Democrats,"
he muttered to no one in particular. "If it's not one thing,
it's always something else. Social Security – humbug!
What will it be next? Some worse cockamamie scheme, no
doubt. If you ask me," which no one in the room did,
"FDR's a stinkin' socialist. Probably let the Bolsheviks
take over if he wins again next fall!"

Grandma Mildred said nothing. She had heard it all before and knew she would hear it again. She had voted to re-elect Herbert Hoover in 1932 but, beyond that, she paid little attention to politics. She considered most of it to be little more than a man's irritating hobby and a waste of time at that. Finished with the monologue, he put the pipe back in his mouth and resumed reading.

Soon it was Lilly's bedtime. "Be sure to say your prayers," Mildred cautioned behind her as the little girl started up the stairs.

"Is it okay to pray to God to ask Santa to bring me a pony for Christmas?" Lilly shot back. "Would that be okay?"

"You can ask him," Harry called out from behind his paper. "Just remember God doesn't always give us everything we ask for."

"I'll remember, Daddy. And I'll be sure to say *pretty please.*"

Now about to turn fourteen, Phillip had a later bedtime than his sister but announced he was tired. He yawned, laid down his magazine and followed her up the steep, narrow stairway.

Harry had finished his paper and refilled his pipe. Katherine had never smoked and, especially as a doctor, had always discouraged it in others. She remembered fondly, however, the aroma of Grandpa's tobacco. The smell of it brought back cherished memories of her time at their house. "The poor thing has her heart so set on a pony," Harry remarked when the children were out of earshot. "It pains me so much that she'll be disappointed

Christmas. Phillip understands that there's no money for the shotgun he wants to go hunting with but little Lilly ..."

Katherine felt a tear run down her cheek.

"I know, Papa." Katherine remembered that Grandma had always called her husband 'Papa' in front of their children and grandchildren. She hardly recalled Grandma calling him *Harry*. "It saddens me, too, but I there isn't much we can do about it."

"Pshaw," Harry replied. "If only there was a way."

Waiting a time until she was sure Lilly was asleep and wouldn't be coming back down the stairs, Mildred brought out her sewing basket and resumed her work on the little dress she was making. It was good that Lilly was still small. It took less of the egg money to buy fabric to make her a new cotton dress for Christmas and there was just enough of the material left over to make a matching dress for her daughter's favorite doll.

Katherine still felt like she was intruding on a private family moment but felt powerless to do anything about it. "But they *are* my family," she rationalized. After another hour or so had passed, Grandma Mildred sighed and put away her sewing.

Grandpa Harry disappeared briefly into the wash-up room and returned with a small armload of wood, which he put into the firebox of the range. Katherine remembered hearing from Mama that the little house had no other source of heat. The brick cellar was small and there was little room for a furnace. Besides, Grandpa had always believed that, were he to put one in, the heat would have spoiled all of the potatoes, onions, and apples stored down there. Anyway, it didn't take much to heat the entire house. There were only two small bedrooms upstairs. Downstairs was the kitchen, and behind that, Grandma and Grandpa's bedroom – no parlor, no dining room. The wash-up room had once been a porch. At some point, it had been enclosed and a cast-iron sink installed along with a hand pump at one end for drawing water from the cistern.

After Grandma and Grandpa retreated to the bedroom and all was dark, Katherine debated whether to stay in kitchen or to go back to the chair in Mama's room. She settled into Grandpa Harry's slightly cushioned armchair beside the stove. Closing her eyes and listening to the crackle of the fire, she fell asleep, no longer concerned about how she had gotten here.

# CHAPTER III

Katherine awoke to the sound of people stirring in the kitchen and the metallic clunk of Grandma's giant cast-iron skillet landing on the range-top. She blearily opened her eyes and saw Grandpa walk in from the wash-up room with an armload of firewood. As she watched, he began placing pieces into the stove's firebox. It was still dark outside. She could not tell if the snow had stopped until Grandpa stepped outside and ducked back in, announcing that it had not. "This one's going to be a real stemwinder,". She had not heard the term "stemwinder" for many years and had nearly forgotten about it. Smiling, she recalled fondly it being one of his favorite expressions to describe anything dramatic, ominous, or exciting. It could refer to weather, a political event, or even sometimes one of Pastor Evans' Sunday sermons.

Even when the sun came up, the clouds and snow hid it from sight. Daylight and dark blended into each other. Regardless, there were chores to be done. "I'm glad it's Saturday," Lilly announced gleefully.

Phillip was less enthusiastic. "Yeah, I guess so," he grumbled. At his age he was expected to fully participate in feeding the horses and hogs, carrying hay to the cattle in the barn lot, and milking the Holsteins. "You're such as sissy," he barked at his sister.

"I'm not a 'sissy', I'm a *girl*. And you're a big brat!" She stuck her tongue out at him, forgetting that later she would have to put on her coat and trek with Grandma Mildred to the henhouse to help feed the chickens and gather eggs.

While Grandma and Lilly cleared away the breakfast dishes, Grandpa Harry ducked out to the wash-up room. He returned with one arm in the sleeve of the red-plaid mackinaw and the other arm partly shoved into the remaining one. "I can't believe that's the same coat!" Katherine knew he could not hear her but she could not help herself. The coat and matching hat with its flannel earflaps looked brand new. "Those had to be so old when I saw them hanging in the storage closet," she chuckled to herself. "The cuffs were so frayed they were nearly gone. I remember those denim patches on the elbows, covering other patches. And that hat!" she laughed. "I can't believe Grandma didn't throw *that* away long before I was born."

Of course, no one who lived through the Great Depression ever really left it behind, she reminded herself – even later when times grew better. She remembered Mama Lilly patching Dad's 'around the house' jeans even when they easily could afford new ones and how he wore them as a badge of honor when working in the yard. "Make it do or do without," she recalled. "Use it up or wear it out." Well, Grandpa sure enough wore out that old coat!

Katherine followed Grandpa and Uncle Phillip out the back door. Since the first night in Mama's room, she had felt neither warm nor cold. They pulled the collars of their coats tightly around their necks and folded their arms closely around them as they trudged toward the barn. Despite being dressed only in her jeans and sweater, she felt perfectly comfortable. Glancing behind her, she gasped in surprise. While Grandpa and Phillip kicked up snow and left tracks, she did not.

Nearing the barn, she suddenly recalled pictures Mama had shown her of Gertrude and Gretchen, Grandpa's great

17

Belgian mares – photographs and a drawing of them that Mama had made when she was little. She still had the drawing in a box at the condo. They had been gone from the farm long before she came along. Anticipation welled up within her that now she might get to see them for herself.

As the barn doors opened, a pungent odor assailed her nostrils. But it also smelt alive, much unlike the stale, arid smell that she recalled from her days playing in the barn as a child. Mama and Daddy would always bring her to the farm soon after school was out. The horses, by that time, were long gone, along with the other inhabitants of the barn. Grandpa still brought cows into the barn to milk them but only two – a Holstein and a Brown Swiss. They provided just enough milk for drinking and cooking and enough cream for Grandma to make her own butter. When not being milked, the cows spent their days in the pasture. The barn, she recalled, had become little more than a giant playhouse for her and for Cousin Jerry, who lived close by. The hay put up the previous summer was mostly gone – carried during the winter to the feedlot or hauled out to pasture to feed the herd of cows carrying the next generation of calves. What stayed on the floor remained year in and year out, dry and dusty, waiting to be covered over by the new crop.

And there were sounds. The only ones she remembered from her childhood were the ones that she and Jerry made as they chased each other around in the empty structure and that of milk hitting the metal pail as Grandpa coaxed it from the two cows. This morning, a cacophony of noises filled the entire barn. She could hear Gertrude and Gretchen even before she saw them. Even with straw bedding in their stalls, their great shod hooves echoed as they stamped the wooden floor. There was a great amount of snorting and the shaking of withers as the pair awaited their morning ration of oats. With the snorting came the exhaling of steam from the horses' nostrils into the cold pre-dawn air.

She spied two cats, curled together on a pile of straw beside one of the feed bins. Obviously worn out from a night of hunting mice, they slept contentedly and ignored the noises around them. One was all black except for a large white spot on its back. The other was an orange tabby whose large left paw covered most of its face. She and David had never owned cats but she recalled Mama talking fondly of her own cats, Ginger and Sally, whom she occasionally tried to sneak into the house and up to her room.

The mare, Gretchen, stretched her great neck over the feed box at the front of her stall. Katherine reached out and stroked the white streak that ran down Gretchen's nose. The horse leaned its head into her as if wanting more. "You felt that, didn't you?" she asked. Gretchen nodded her head as if agreeing. As she did so, Katherine reached closer and began to gently stroke the great beast's ears. "No, surely not." Yet the horse seemed to respond to her name. She soon realized that Gretchen was responding not to her own touch, but to Phillip's. Disappointed, she stepped back to watch.

As Katherine tried making friends with Gretchen and then with Gertrude, Grandpa Harry made his way toward the milking stall. He stopped suddenly when he noticed a light coming from near the stanchions. He approached slowly and observed that two of the cows were already in place awaiting their turn. "Who's there?" Katherine heard him call out. She moved quickly toward the stall to see what was going on and then remembered the story her mother had related to her many years ago.

"My name's George, George Albers". The man stood up, partly obscured by the Holstein.

"Stay where you are," Harry commanded. "What are you doing here?"

"I'm sorry," George answered haltingly. "I didn't mean to trespass. Honestly, I didn't. I just needed a warm place to sleep. I was hoping that if I brought the cows in for you to milk, you might give me a little something to eat."

Harry was struck by the man's small stature. His head barely showed above the cow's hips. "You can come on out," Harry assured him. "No one's going to hurt you."

"Where did you come from?" Harry continued. "How long have you been here?"

"Since about seven or so last night, as far as I can tell. The train slowed down at the bridge down yonder and I got kicked off for hoboing. I saw the light coming from your house and figured there must be a barn where I could get out of the snow. I didn't see any harm in it."

"You could have come to the house," Phillip chimed in. "Couldn't he, Dad?"

Harry started to respond but George spoke first. "Tried that other times. It didn't go well. I just figured I'd stay here overnight. Hoped to maybe get a little something to eat and then move on. There aren't many colored folks around these parts and I didn't think white folks would take too kindly to a colored beggar showing up at their door in the middle of the night."

"Well, when we finish here, we'll take you to the house and get some coffee and some hot food in your belly. Have you ever milked a cow?"

For the first time in their encounter, George flashed a smile. "Nearly all my life. I grew up on a dairy farm in Wisconsin - milked every day almost from the time I was big enough to reach the teats. When I turned eighteen, I joined the army and went to France."

Harry handed him a bucket. "Then grab a stool and a cow! By the way, I'm Harry Heath and this is my son, Phillip."

When they returned to the house, Harry introduced George to Mildred and Lilly. Mildred welcomed him openly and offered him a seat at the table. Lilly just stared. Finally, she spoke. "Why is your …?

"Don't, Mama!" Katherine exclaimed, even though she knew Lilly couldn't hear her words of caution. "Don't say it."

Grandma Mildred chimed in also but it was too late.

"Why is your skin all brown like that? Were you out in the sun too long? Daddy gets kinda' like that in the summer when he works in the fields."

"Lilly!"

"It's alright Ma'am," George spoke softly. "The little one's probably never seen a colored man before. "It's like this, Lilly. You have red hair and freckles, right?"

"Yes," she answered shyly."

"And it's very pretty red hair and pretty freckles. Tell me. Do all of you friends have red hair and freckles?"

"Of course not. Some have brown hair and some have blonde hair and most don't have freckles."

"And that's how it works." George leaned forward in his chair and put his hands on his knees. "You see, God made all of us different so we could each be special. He gave you pretty red hair and freckles and he gave me dark brown skin but then, inside, he made us all the same."

Lilly was satisfied and cautiously approached him. At arm's length, she stopped, put her hands behind her back, and looked up at him. "Well, I think you're very handsome!"

"Why thank you, Lilly. You're a very polite little girl. I think your mommy and daddy should be very proud of you."

Katherine felt herself tearing up.

No one said much as George ate the bacon and eggs. Harry expected him dig in ravenously and gorge himself. Instead, he ate slowly and politely. Harry had already decided that George was a gentleman.

"Thank you, Ma'am. That was the best meal I've had in ages. I'll be on my way now. You've all been mighty good to me but I don't want to intrude on your kindness."

George's clothes were ragged and hung loosely on his small frame but Harry could tell they had not always been that way. "You needn't be in a hurry to go, George. We don't feel intruded on. If I can ask, and you don't have to say if you don't want, where did you come from before you hopped that train?"

"Oh, I've been around but I haven't always been a hobo. A man just does what he needs to do to get by. That's what I've been doing for, I guess, nigh on to a year or so now. Just going from town to town or farm to farm looking for work in exchange for my next meal. Some folks wouldn't even talk to me. Some would feed me and give me a little food to take along but then tell me I had to be on my way. You're the first who actually invited me in.

Anyhow, you asked where I came from. Remember, I told you out in the barn that I grew up on a dairy farm in Wisconsin. Then I joined the army and went to France in the war. We coloreds weren't allowed to fight alongside white fellows, of course. Many of us were cooks and such. I was a wagon driver and my best friend was a blacksmith. When I came back, I decided I wanted to do something other than farm so I went down to Alabama and enrolled in Tuskegee Institute. That's a college mostly for black men."

"I'm familiar with it."

"I decided I wanted to be a teacher and help other colored folks to better themselves. After I graduated, I found a job teaching manual arts and music at a high school near Chicago. I did that all through the 20's – never found the right girl to marry, never had kids but I managed to support myself pretty well. Then, with the depression, the principal's cousin came along one day needing a teaching job so the principal gave him mine."

"That's awful!" Mildred exclaimed.

"Well, I guess that's just the way of the world, Ma'am. I try never to be bitter so I just moved on. I got a job, close your ears little one, killing cattle at the stockyards but only worked there a few days. The noise and the blood and all

23

reminded me too much of the war so I left. I tried finding a teaching job at another school but no one was hiring. So that's when I hopped my first freight and started travelling all around trying to find chores to do so I could eat."

Lilly, having lost her shyness, walked up to him and wrapped her arms around his leg. "My daddy used to play music."

"Lilly."

"Then he had to sell his guitar to buy seed to plant the crops last spring."

"Lilly."

"He's gonna get a new one soon though. I'm asking Santa Claus to bring him a new one. I'm asking him to bring Mama a sewing machine and Phillip a shotgun so he can go hunting."

"You're a very thoughtful little girl, Lilly," George told her. "And what are you asking Santa to bring you?"

"I'm asking him for a pony," she replied. "But I think Santa maybe doesn't bring ponies. So, just in case, I'm asking for a doll cradle, too."

# CHAPTER IV

By evening, the snow had tapered to a few lonely flakes
flitting about. By nightfall the moon and the stars had
appeared, illuminating the farmyard in its soft, white light.
The departure of the clouds brought with it a bone-chilling
cold, pushed forth by a loudly howling north wind. Lilly
had long since gone to bed while Phillip sat at the kitchen
table, engrossed in a Zane Grey novel a friend had loaned
him. As Mildred safely tucked away the doll dress she had
been sewing, Harry knocked out the cold ashes from his
pipe and headed to the wash-up room for wood to stoke the
stove for overnight. George followed him, heading toward
the back door.

"Where are you going, George?"

"Well, you've all been very kind," George answered. "I just
thought, if it's alright with you, I'd hole up in your barn for
the night. Then, come morning, I'll gather up my things
that I left out there and be on my way.

"You can't sleep in the barn," Harry retorted.

George gave him an unbelieving look. "But I ..."

"But nothing, George," Harry quickly interrupted. "You
can't sleep in the barn because it's too cold. Mildred and I
could never forgive ourselves if you were sleeping out
there when it's warm and safe here in the house." He
reached behind an old wardrobe stacked with empty
canning jars and other assorted utensils, and pulled out a
worn, but still sturdy, folding canvas cot. "We'll get you a

couple of blankets and you can sleep here next to the sink. It's not much but it's better than out there."

"Why not bring the cot up to my room," Phillip called out from kitchen. "I can use the company!"

"Then it's settled, George. Come this way."

Since it was Sunday, the family rose earlier than usual. The morning chores all had to be done before breakfast. After breakfast, Grandma and Lilly washed the dishes while Grandpa hitched Gertrude and Gretchen to the box sleigh. All this had to be done before everyone changed into their Sunday best and then bundled up for the three-mile ride to Church.

Katherine followed Grandpa, Phillip, and George. Although the snow had stopped, the wind continued to howl, lifting and driving the biting cold snowfall into their faces as they walked. They trudged silently toward the barn, shovels in hand. The wind had created drifts that rose nearly to the building's eaves, entirely blocking the entrance.

Inside, they were again met by an odd symphony of animal noises as the creatures made their needs known. Gretchen and Gertrude stamped their hooves and snorted heavily as they waited for hay to be thrown into the troughs in the front of their stalls. From his own stall, Fred the mule brayed impatiently. Blackjack, the Angus cross-breed bull named after Grandpa's hero, General Blackjack Pershing, joined in the fray, bellowing loudly. The cows, brought in from the cold last night, were a bit more subdued but clearly anxious to be fed and relieved of their milk.

"George," Harry asked as they set about their work, "why don't you come to church with us?"

"I appreciate the invitation, I really do, but I'm not sure your friends would be entirely comfortable with a colored man suddenly showing up in their midst. No, I think it's best if I just do my Sunday morning praying here. By the way, what's wrong with Mrs. Heath's sewing machine? I'm guessing its broken since she's doing her sewing by hand and the little one is asking Santa Claus to bring her a new one."

"I don't really know. It just quit working a few weeks back. I've looked at it but haven't been able to find any faults with it. The foot treadle is stuck but I don't know why. It's got to be something set in the machine itself. There isn't anyone in town who works on them and, even if there was, it would cost money I don't have."

"I've been known to tinker with stuff," George replied. "Sometimes, I'm even able to fix things. If you have some tools, maybe I could have a look at it while she's at church. If I'm able to fix it, maybe keep it a secret and surprise her with it at Christmas."

"That would be a wonderful thing to do George. We'll make sure she knows you're the one who fixed it for her."

Afterwards, Katherine watched Grandpa and George hitch the horses to the box sleigh. There was an aged Model "T" Ford in the machinery shed next to the barn but she remembered Mama saying Grandpa rarely drove it in those days. "It was always needing repairs," Mama had told her. "There wasn't much money to spare for gasoline. They didn't use it at all in the snow. The drifts made it too dangerous and it got stuck too easily."

Katherine watched enviously as the family piled into the sleigh. Grandpa sat alone on the seat so he could drive the team while the rest of the family snuggled together in the back, covered with layers of blankets. She longed to see the old church again and the long-gone faces of Grandpa and Grandma's friends. As with her grandparents, she only remembered them as elderly with white hair and canes. She remembered hands shaking as they held their hymnals, some unable to stand as they sang. How wonderful to be able to see them all in their prime, healthy and vibrant! Most of all, she wished she could hear Grandpa sing while Grandma played the piano. She had heard Grandma play when she visited as a child but a strep infection had ruined Grandpa's tenor voice long before she was born. The only thing holding her back from going with them was fear. She wasn't sure how she'd been transported to this time and place and was afraid what might happen if she left the farm. "No, it was better not to chance it."

Reluctantly, she returned to the wash-up room, and watched George begin to examine the sewing machine. First, he crawled under and checked the treadle and its connection to the driving rod. He admired the machine's craftsmanship as he felt around for connections that had either come loose or gotten jammed. Next, he lifted the machine's head using the hinges that secured it to the cabinet. He hoped there weren't broken parts that he couldn't fix or 'jerry-rig' since he would be unable to actually replace them with new ones. Mildred wouldn't know the difference since she wasn't aware what he was doing but he knew Harry would be disappointed if he couldn't put the machine back in order.

The week passed quickly for the rest of the family but much too slowly for Lilly, who could think only of Christmas and a visit from Santa Claus. Each day, after school, she would eagerly relate to her mother what Miss Ellen had read from *National Velvet* and ask Grandpa if it was time to fetch the Christmas tree. With each passing day, George became more a part of the family. He not only helped with daily chores around the barn but also split firewood and assisted with various other tasks. He developed a special bond with Phillip as they discussed articles from *Popular Mechanics*. Phillip especially liked hearing about how George had actually seen Charles Lindbergh and his plane, the *Spirit of St. Louis* when the famed aviator made a countrywide tour after his adventurous flight to Paris.

Finally, it was Saturday morning once more. Grandpa took a saw from the wash-up room and summoned Lilly to accompany him to bring in the Christmas tree. She eagerly put on her coat, mittens, and galoshes and trailed after him into the snow toward the gate to the timber. As soon as they had left, George asked Phillip to come with him to the barn. Katherine curiously followed along, torn between watching their secret rendezvous or joining the Christmas tree expedition.

Just outside the milking room was a shaft that led to the hayloft. It was used to throw hay and straw bedding back down to the main floor. As Phillip and Katherine watched, George stepped in and began to climb the built-in ladder. "Wait there. I'll be right back." Moments later, George's feet re-appeared, followed shortly after by a large black leather case, which he handed to Phillip. "Here. Take this so I can get on down. Thanks, Come with me."

In the harness and tool room, George laid the case on the work bench and opened it. Though the case showed wear from years of being carried around, the guitar it contained did not. To the astonished Phillip, it appeared brand new, as if it had never been played. "Wow! Can I touch it?"

"May I," George gently corrected him. "And yes, you may. Have you ever played before?"

"Daddy tried a couple of times to teach me but I never really got the hang of it. I guess I'm just not made for music. I think that made him sad since he's so good at it."

"That's alright young man. We all have our different talents. I'm sure he recognizes that even if he doesn't say it much. I can tell he's proud of you. I'm thinking you're really good with tools."

"Next fall, when I start high school, they have classes in manual arts. I'm looking forward to that."

"You'll do just fine."

"Why did you keep this hidden up in the hayloft though?"

"Oh, it wasn't always up there. That first night I came here, I just tucked it under some straw. When your daddy invited me into the house, I forgot about it. When Lilly said he had to sell his to buy seed and I got invited to stay a while, I came up with a different plan. First chance I got, I snuck back out here and hid it up there. I want to give it to him for Christmas."

"He'd love that but are you sure you want …?"

"Oh, yes," George assured him. "I'm very sure. Let me tell you something about this old guitar. You see, it belonged to my own papa. He gave it to me when I came home from the army and went off to college. He died a few years later and this is the only thing I have left that was his. When I started jumping trains, I played it for folks who were kind enough to give me some work and some food. Honestly, there weren't a lot of them, but there were some. None of 'em were ever as kind as your parents. They were surely the first folks who ever offered to take me in. So, that's why I want to give it to your daddy.

I need you to do something for me, Phillip. First chance you get, I need you to sneak this into the house and hide it under your bed."

"Sure thing," Phillip answered. "I need a favor too."

"What's that?"

"It's a week 'til Christmas. I need you to help me make Lilly a doll cradle."

Katherine watched from the kitchen window as Mama and Grandpa came proudly up the lane. Grandpa had the pine tree slung over his back, its tip leaving a jagged line in the snow behind him. Lilly skipped merrily ahead, singing *Jingle Bells* and waving her arms back and forth in mirth. Grandma greeted them at the door and looked in amazement at the size of the tree. She wasn't one to dampen anyone's spirits but, in this case, she couldn't help herself. "For heaven's sake, Papa! Have you lost your mind? That tree is huge. Just where in our little house do you plan to put it?" She looked down at Lilly who seemed as though she was about to cry. With a sigh, Grandma conceded, "Alright, bring it on in. We'll make it work somehow."

Moments later, Phillip and George arrived back from the barn. Lilly helped Grandma remove everything from the icebox so the men could carry it to the wash-up room. That made space to put the tree in the kitchen in its place. When the move was complete and the icebox reloaded, Lilly disappeared up the stairs. She returned with a wooden box that had once contained saltine crackers. It was now filled with stars that she had carefully cut out from used tinfoil and tied together with red string. Grandpa headed to the barn and returned with a large metal bucket used to feed oats to the horses and Fred. George fashioned a stand which he placed in the bucket along with sand and water to keep the tree's needles green and fresh until after Christmas.

Harry, George, and Phillip spent the rest of the afternoon splitting firewood for the stove and re-stocking the lean-to behind the smokehouse. Meanwhile, Mildred and Lilly busied themselves with popping fresh popcorn and stringing it to wrap around the tree. "Mama, Daddy doesn't smoke his pipe anymore, does he?"

"No, sweetheart."

"Doesn't he like it? I think it smells good."

"He still likes it, Lilly. It makes him feel better when he has things to worry about. But he has run out of tobacco and there isn't any money to buy more so he's given it up 'til times get better."

"What things does he worry about, Mama?"

Mildred wished she hadn't mentioned it. "He worries 'bout grown-up things that little girls needn't worry themselves about."

"But it makes him sad, doesn't it?"

"Yes, sometimes."

"I want to make him happy."

"Oh, sweetie, you do make him happy. Whenever he tells you stories or watches you play or kisses you goodnight, it makes him very happy."

"I know, Mama, but I mean I want to do something to make him *really, really* happy."

"Tell you what. When he comes back in, you just give him a big ol' hug and kiss him on the cheek. That'll perk him right up like nobody's business!"

"I will Mama. And I'll give you one, too – and Phillip and George, I mean *Mister Albers*"

"We'd all like that, Lilly. And just for starters, you can give your Mama one now."

"Me, too," Katherine commented unheard. "I guess I'll just have to wait awhile longer for mine though."

"Mama?" Lilly sidled closer.

"Yes, sweetie."

"How much does Daddy's tobacco cost?"

After dinner, Lilly sat on her father's lap and looked at the Christmas tree as George and Phillip engaged in a lively game of checkers at the kitchen table. Her eyes sparked with joy. "Daddy, I wish you still had your guitar so you could make Christmas music for us." George gave Phillip a furtive, knowing smile.

"Well, little one, tell you what." He pulled her closer. "Since you're such a good girl, I'll sing to you even without a guitar."

Katherine's heart nearly burst with joy. It was the moment she had been hoping for but wasn't sure would come. Everything else in the room stopped. It looked to Katherine like a Christmas card or Norman Rockwell painting – the quaint tree, the checker game, the shadows from the kerosene lamp dancing on the ceiling, the light shining through the range's grate from the crackling wood burning within. And then, as they all held their breath, Grandpa began to sing. *"Away in a manger, no crib for a bed, the little Lord Jesus lay down his sweet head..."*

Soon it was time for bed. Phillip, George, and Lilly yawned and headed upstairs while Harry brought in more wood to stoke the fire for the night. Mildred carried the lamp to their bedroom. "I have good news," Harry told her softly a little later, so Phillip and Lilly would not hear. "Ralph Grainge has told me they are moving to Chicago. That's not the good news though," he added. "They've been good neighbors and we'll miss them for sure. The good news is that Francie has outgrown her pony and was barely riding him anymore anyhow. They want to give him to Lilly. Ralph's going to bring him over Christmas Eve and we'll keep him in the barn. If the weather's decent Christmas morning, I'll bring him out and tie him up near the back door when I finish chores."

"Harry, that's wonderful!" She almost shouted and ruined the surprise.

"There's more." The dim light hid his wide grin but she could hear his excitement anyway. "Sam Edwards wants to repay me for repairing those two harnesses last fall. He asked what he could do. I told him just 'thanks' was enough and I meant it. But it occurred to me the other day that he used to repair guns back when he was in the war. I asked him if could fix up Dad's old shotgun for Phillip and he said he was pretty sure he could. I just need to get it to him without Phillip finding out. When Phillip and I are in town tomorrow, maybe you could call him and he can drop over and pick it up."

"You're a wonderful papa! The children will be so happy."

"You will be, too," he told himself softly before dropping off to sleep.

Phillip awoke suddenly when Lilly jabbed him in ribs. He rolled over quickly and saw her standing by his bed. "Lilly! What did you do that for?!"

George was a sound sleeper. On his cot on the other side of the small room, he heard nothing.

"I need to talk to you."

He leaned up on his elbow. "About what? Can't it wait until morning?"

"Uh, uh," she protested.

"Okay then, what is it?" He sat up on the bed and motioned for her to sit beside him.

"Daddy doesn't smoke his pipe anymore."

"No."

"Do you know why?"

"I haven't given it much thought, Lilly. Honestly, I haven't really paid much attention."

"Mama says he doesn't have any money for tobacco anymore."

"Yeah, well …"

"You and Daddy are gonna walk to town tomorrow, right?"

"Yes. He says he has to pick up Mama's Christmas surprise from a shop there."

Katherine had followed Lilly when she tiptoed out and now watched as she pulled out a small cardboard box from within her nightgown. Opening it, Lilly revealed the contents to Phillip. "But, Lilly, that's all of your allowance. You've been saving that for ages."

Katherine looked into the box. It was nearly bare but contained a small assortment of pennies, a few nickels, even fewer dimes and two quarters.

"I was gonna use it to buy some butterscotch candy but I think Daddy needs his pipe tobacco more. Mama said when he smokes his pipe, he doesn't worry about things as much."

Phillip dutifully took the box and set it on the night table, knowing what he would do with it. "Go back to sleep, Lilly. Everything will be alright."

# CHAPTER V

Right after breakfast, Harry and Phillip bundled up and walked down the lane, headed for town. George walked to the shop in the barn and began scavenging for wood to make a start on the doll cradle. Katherine watched as Grandma walked to the telephone and turned the crank. As she waited for the operator, she turned to Lilly and raised her finger to her lips. "This is a secret for Phillip," she said. "You need to promise not to tell him."

"I promise, Mama."

By mid-afternoon, the delicious aroma of gingerbread cookies, an apple pie, and fresh bread wafted throughout the kitchen. By lunchtime, George had finished work for the day. Since Harry's chair was unoccupied and the kitchen table was full, he chose a book from the shelf and lounged there, trying his best to stay out of the way.

It was nearly time for the evening chores when Harry and Phillip finally came trudging back up the lane, subtly making a detour to the barn. By the time Grandma and Lilly noticed, they were only carrying only a cardboard box containing a few items that had been requested from the grocery and a two-gallon glass jug of kerosene. They talked little, both out of breath from their long hike in the cold, but both solidly pleased with the fruits of their journey.

Tuesday morning was Christmas Eve. The weather had started out pleasantly but by mid-morning, the temperature had dropped to nearly zero and it had begun to snow. Lilly was nearly crazy with anticipation. The day couldn't arrive quickly enough. Tonight, Santa Claus would come. She had been good. The whole family had been good. She just *knew* that her daddy would get a new guitar, Mama would get a sewing machine, and Phillip would get a shotgun. She looked forward to watching Daddy opening the pipe tobacco that Phillip had secreted back. How Santa could get all of these wonderful things on his sleigh and into the house never crossed her mind.

She also looked forward to finally opening the gift that Miss Ellen had given her on the last day of school. She had wanted to open it right there and then but Miss Ellen insisted that she wait until Christmas. There was no doubt that it was a book but what would it be? Perhaps a Nancy Drew mystery? Or the Bobbsey Twins? Maybe even her own copy of *National Velvet*? And what would Phillip's book be?

It troubled her that she hadn't been able to think of anything to ask Santa to bring for George. Whenever she asked him what he wanted for Christmas, he had simply told her a home-cooked meal and a warm place to sleep were everything he needed. She hoped that he would stay after Christmas and not hop on a train and leave.

Phillip was less excited. He was enjoying having a few days off from school but he knew there would be no hunting gun. It was far beyond the family's means. He may as well have asked for the moon. He looked forward to watching the others receive their gifts though – for Lilly, her doll cradle and butterscotch candy, for Mama, her dress fabric and for Daddy, his guitar and pipe tobacco. Like Lilly, he was disappointed that George seemed to want nothing. Then he remembered that everyone in the family except George had their own Bible. He knew what he needed to do. He would get himself another one someday.

By the time the family was ready to pile into the box-sleigh and leave for Christmas Eve church, the snow had stopped falling. While it was still cold and windy, the clouds had dispersed and the moon and stars had come out, bathing the farm in moonlight. Lilly looked up in wonder. "Mama, which one do you think is Baby Jesus' star?"

"I'm not sure sweetie. I think it's whichever one you like best. God made all of them so it's hard for us to know which one he made especially for Jesus."

They all wanted Harry to sing on the way to church but the cold air made it hard to keep his breath. The wool plaid scarf smothered his mouth and nose, making it impossible to hear him anyhow. Instead, they contented themselves to listening to the jingle of bells from Gretchen's and Gertrude's harness.

George had again protested the invitation to come along but finally gave in to Harry's insistence. Harry didn't want to give away the surprise but convinced George that something very special was going to happen and that he really needed to be there. Katherine also was reluctant but decided to take the chance and tag along. She hated to leave them but knew she would never forget. She knew, now, that Christmas would be wonderful for all of them. It no longer mattered so much to her whether she stayed or went 'home' to Chicago.

The little white clapboard church looked much as Katherine remembered it. But since her childhood visits to Grandpa and Grandma had always been in the summer, she had never seen it like this. It sat in the middle of nowhere, miles from any other shop or homestead. To one side stood a large grove of pine trees, their boughs laden down with heavy snow, drooping low and nearly touching the ground. The moonlight shone on the snow like a million white lights. On the other side was the cemetery, the headstones each topped with snowfall. The entire scene gave the appearance of a crowd of short white-haired observers, silently watching over the proceedings.

Numerous families were arriving, tethering their teams to the hitching rails as they merrily greeted each other. Steam puffed from the horses' nostrils, rising upward to join the smoke drifting from the church's red brick chimney. Harry spied Gerald "Dutch" Kinder and waved to catch his attention. He turned to George. "Come with me. There's someone here who's anxious to meet you."

The distant cousins greeted each other warmly. "Dutch, this is George, our new friend I've been telling you about." He turned to George Albers. "George, this is Dutch Kinder. Dutch is the principal at the local high school. He has a problem I told him I think you can solve. You see, Dutch's manual arts teacher has had to move down south to help take care of his ailing mother."

Katherine walked into church with everyone else. She could hardly contain her excitement, gaily clapping her hands in excitement and calling out to the people she recognized from her childhood visits. Then they had been old or middle-aged, but here they were, young and thriving. Some, she hardly recognized but others she knew instantly. Here were Everett and Mabel Hill. Here were John and Hazel Hardy. She paid little attention to the sermon but since no one could hear her anyway, she exuberantly joined in with the singing of "Silent Night" and the other hymns.

Another who barely heard the sermon was Lilly. Like Katherine, she joined in joyfully with the hymns, but her thoughts were mostly for Santa's visit and tomorrow morning. Lilly stood facing the front of the church but, for a brief moment, Katherine thought she saw Mama turn back to her with a wink and smile. Surprised, she glanced back, but the moment was gone and once again Lilly's attention was on the pastor.

Despite the excitement, Katherine was relieved when she finally arrived back at the house with the family. There had been laughter and chatter all the way home. Lilly was especially bubbly as she cuddled up to George. "I'm so happy you got a job, Mr. Albers."

"You can call me George, little one. I'm just George."

Although she had begun to think of him as Uncle George, it had never occurred to her to call him by his first name.

"Does that mean you'll be staying with us?"

"Well, probably not *with* you, Lilly, since I'll be able to afford my own place now but I promise I'll be nearby and I'll come and visit you and Phillip and your mommy and daddy. And you can all come and visit me anytime."

"I'd like that, George," Lilly added almost shyly.

Katherine watched soulfully as Grandpa and Grandma tucked Lilly into bed and kissed her goodnight. She sat down in the chair in Lilly's room. There was a bit of a draft from the window but it was neither cool nor warm.

When she awoke, it was still dark but Lilly's bed was empty. The sounds of laughter and joyful chatter drifted upstairs and into the room. Distantly, she heard the strumming of a guitar and Grandpa's wonderful singing voice. Then Lilly's excited laughter. "A pony! Santa brought me a pony! Oh, I just knew he would!"

Still groggy with sleep, Katherine rose, walked to the window and pulled back the curtains. It was still snowing but dawn had begun to break over Lake Michigan. She walked to the living room where she had been sitting with the laptop but first made a stop at the bookshelf. She pulled down a small, worn, green-covered volume. *The Little House on the Prairie* by Laura Ingalls Wilder. She opened the cover and read from the flyleaf. *To Lilly Heath from your teacher, Miss Ellen. Christmas 1935.*

She was in a haze, dazed and confused, unsure of what had just happened. Had it all been a wonderful dream? Had she actually gone back and seen them all for real? How long had it been? Did that really matter?

Her coffee was ready. She took a quick sip and went back to the sofa and sat down. The words came easily as she typed. *Dear Jerry, please don't do anything with Grandpa and Grandma's house yet. I have an idea for it. I've decided to come for a visit after all. I'll tell you what I have in mind when I get there.*

*Love you and see you soon.*

*Kate.*

# PART II:

# A HEATH FAMILY CHRISTMAS REUNION

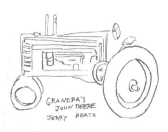

GRANDPA'S
JOHN DEERE
JERRY HEATH

# CHAPTER VI

Katherine Jean, *Adams* since last week, looked out the window of the condo. The sun was just peeking over Lake Michigan but was mostly obscured by the storm that had passed over Iowa and into Illinois overnight. She cupped a mug of fresh hot coffee in her hands as she basked in a hug from behind. "Happy almost first Thanksgiving," her new husband whispered warmly in her ear.

"The first of many I hope," she answered without turning around. "I love you so much. I'm so happy." In some ways, it seemed such a short time. It was less than a year ago since she had stood transfixed at her bedroom window before finding herself 'transported' to the strange but comforting time and place where Mama Lilly was only seven years old. In other ways, it seemed an eternity. She still missed David but was comforted that Keith was so understanding. They shared a common bond. For her, it was only a year and a few months. For Keith, it was nearing five years.

She kissed his cheek, moved to the sofa, and rested her feet on the coffee table. "So, are you nervous about meeting my relatives next month?"

"Not really," he teased. "If they are anything like my new bride, I'm sure they're perfect in nearly every fashion. If anything, you're the one who should be worried when they see what you've brought home."

She gave him a loving swat on the shoulder and laughed. "Oh, yeah. You're a real piece alright. Did you just insult my taste in men?"

"Not at all, sweetheart," he shot back. "I'm just amazed that someone as young and pretty as you would hook up with a white-haired old codger like me."

She stroked his soft, well-groomed white beard. "Well, you're a pretty good cook and you keep me warm at night. You play a pretty mean piano too, by the way."

"A gray, crotchety pianist. How could they not love me?"

"It's not *you* I'm worried about, silly"

"I'm anxious to see what you've done with your grandparents' house. It was an enormous job to restore it to look like it did in the nineteen-fifties.

"I'm anxious for you to see it too. In fact, I'm pretty anxious to see it myself. The pictures the contractor and designer sent yesterday look great but it's still not the same as actually being there." She opened the lid of the laptop computer. "Let's look at them again."

"How much of it were you actually able to save?"

"I was surprised at how much was still usable, really. The house was a lot more solid than Jerry led me to believe. I can't tell you how much I appreciate your help in hunting down all of the correct furniture and appliances. I really wanted it to look just right. I'm so lucky to have married an antique hunter." She gave him a peck on the cheek. "Old things really *are* valuable. It looks just like it did when I was little! And that flowered wallpaper! How on earth did you ...?"

"This is Chicago, my darling. Between Chicago and the internet, you can find anything."

She clapped her hands together. "I'm so excited!"

"Shall we drive out there and see it?"

"I'm tempted but I think it'll be more fun to wait until we're ready to decorate it for Christmas. I'm getting tingles, though"

"Do you know what *I'm* getting", he asked?

"No. What are you getting?"

"Hungry!"

"Good. Then you can fix breakfast for us both! I'll have a Denver omelet, extra spicy."

\*\*\*\*

Mildred Heath looked around. Her farmhouse kitchen was just as she remembered it in 1955. Even the calendar advertising the Burkeville Creamery was right. It featured a picture of a white-country church against a background of a grassy meadow lined with pine trees. Thanksgiving was highlighted in red. The hard times of the 1930's had given way to the current prosperity. Kerosene lamps were stored away, only to be brought out in case of a power outage. Instead, a three-bulb ceiling fixture provided instant light at the touch of a button. The cast iron stove that had cooked all of the meals and provided heat for the entire home was long gone. It had been replaced by a Hotpoint electric range. A propane furnace in the basement underneath the room addition provided steady warmth and didn't need stoked at night. When the Rural Electrification Administration lines first reached the farm eight years before, the oak icebox had immediately lost its spot to a gleaming white Frigidaire refrigerator. The Hoosier cabinet with its tambour roll and built-in flour sifter now sat in the wash-up room, filled with rarely used odds and ends. It had been replaced by white cupboards over blue Formica countertops Where once there had been a round oak table, there was now one with chrome legs and a Formica top that matched the counter tops. It was surrounded by four chairs with blue vinyl backs and seats. A similar oak table with cane chairs now occupied the space that had been their bedroom until they added onto the home after the war and turned the old bedroom into dining room. It all seemed so real that she expected to see little Katherine rush in from the wash-up room with her parents, Lilly and Ed, close behind. She held out her arms expectantly. Sadly, she pulled them back empty.

She walked to the sink and remembered how she had marveled when she could first could obtain water by simply turning the handle on a faucet. She stared out the window toward the barn. The wind drove a wispy, powdery snow across the porch roof, causing it to whirl like a small tornado before hurrying on its way to make room for the next gust. The sky was tinged a slight orange against the backdrop of barren tree branches.

With a heavy sigh, she turned and headed up the narrow stairway into what had once been her son Phillip's bedroom but was now hers and Harry's. She reached through the lace curtains, giving a small tug to the green roll-up shade. "Harry, wake up!"

****

Jerry Heath lounged in a deck chair and surveyed the blue waters of the Gulf of Mexico. He would have preferred swimming in the gulf rather than the condo's pool but, even though it was only mid-November, the water was already a bit cool for his taste. He loved coming here in the winters with Janice. It brought him a sense of closeness with his father, Phillip. Naval Air Station Pensacola, after all, was only a few miles down the road. He remembered Dad's stories of his time there as an aviation cadet in the months following Pearl Harbor. The planes of Dad's day, of course, were long gone. But, in the quiet hours when the jet fighters weren't flying, he could close his eyes and imagine a sky filled with prop-driven trainers, manned by student pilots who would soon be headed to the Pacific.

They did not miss at all getting up on cold, snowy mornings to do chores around the barn or haul hay out for the cattle. They had decided five years ago that winter on the farm was for younger people. Their son, Alan, his wife Theresa, and the grandchildren seemed content with their life back in Iowa. He missed them but Christmas was coming and he would see them soon enough. Then, of course, spring and summer would arrive. He could help Alan with the farm and Janice loved assisting Theresa with the vegetable and flower gardens. This would be Tommy's first year showing 4-H market lambs and Elaine's first as a teenager. He sipped his orange juice and savored the afterglow of his morning swim. "Life is good," he murmured with a smile.

He placed the juice on the side-table and opened the laptop. "Janice," he shouted through the open sliders to the kitchen. "Come look at this! Kate sent pictures. I have to give her credit. Honestly, I never thought she'd actually pull it off. It looks amazing!"

They moved to the bistro table and pulled up chairs so they could look together. "Oh my gosh! It looks just like it did when I was a kid!" Starting with the wash-up room, they marveled over the details. Grandma and Grandpa had kept the cast iron sink and hand pump even after they acquired running water in the kitchen. It remained a convenient way to wash off hay chaff, sweat, and chore grime without dirtying either the kitchen or the bathroom. The electric cream separator and the chest-type food freezer looked just as he remembered, as did Grandma's Maytag wringer washer. "There's even a Roy Rogers lunchbox!"

They scrolled through the kitchen pictures next. A Philco radio sat on small shelf near the wall-mounted telephone with its hand crank and corded earpiece.

"I remember when I finally got big enough to stand on a stool and talk to Mom over at our house. Of course, you couldn't talk for long because all of Grandma's friends wanted in on the party line."

"Guess she didn't need Facebook."

"Nope. Everyone knew everyone else's business without it. You don't know what you missed, city girl!"

Burkeville, with its five hundred people, wasn't exactly a city but she knew what he meant.

"That house wasn't much different than ours was when Mom and Dad built it," he continued, "except ours was larger and the living and dining rooms were built in instead of added on later. Still, there was the magic of being at Grandma's – and there were cookies!"

Those kitchen counters!" Jerry remarked. "Grandma used to let me pull out her breadboard and all of the pots and pans underneath. I didn't play with them but I would crawl into the space and pretend I was an aviator flying in the war like Dad. When I told her what I was playing, she didn't like it but she didn't scold me either. She told me how she and Grandpa always worried that he wouldn't come home. Since he *did* come home, I don't think she really minded my play as much as she let on."

"Speaking of the living room add-on ..."

"I can't wait to get in there," he interrupted. "It looks like it has everything but Grandpa and Grandma themselves!"

****

Alan, finished the last few bites of ham and eggs and picked up his cell phone. "Hey, Theresa, we have an e-mail from Katherine. She sent pictures of the house!"

"Finally!"

The whole process had been shrouded in secrecy. It had been nearly a year since Dad had instructed him not to tear down the house. Then, late last winter, Jerry had sold the small acreage to his cousin, Katherine. Soon, grading had begun on a new road that bypassed the little farmstead to provide alternate access to the corn and soybean fields. Shortly after that, the contractors arrived to shore up and restore the house that he had long-considered to be unsalvageable. Jerry had sold the place reluctantly but now both he and Alan had to admit that the whole idea intrigued them. No one except Katherine and the workers had stepped inside. From the moment the contractors finished their work on the outside, the window blinds were pulled and the house marked as completely off-limits. There had been many times last summer when Jerry and Janice were back home, that everyone had been tempted to take a sneak peek. But it was Katherine's house now to do with as she wished. She was normally a kind and gentle soul but none

50

of them wanted to chance incurring her wrath. "All in due time," she had warned. "You'll all see it when I'm ready for you to, and not a moment before."

# CHAPTER VII

"Ah! Come on, Bears. You're better than that!" Keith Adams shouted at the TV. "Geez. In college, I could have completed that pass in my sleep!

Katherine sat beside him and laughed. The condo was comfortably warm but they had turned the heat down as an excuse to sit by the fireplace and snuggle under a fleece blanket. They had just finished their Thanksgiving dinner and curled up on the sofa. She was glad she hadn't yet sipped her wine. She was sure she would have spit it out in her laughter. "You old horse! You played trombone in the band at halftime!" she reminded him. "Remember? I was there!"

"Well, yeah, but, if I had played ..."

"If you had played," she interrupted, "they would have killed you!"

"You're kind of snippety for such a new wife," he teased.

"Well, I may be a new wife but it's not like I haven't known you for fifty-plus years!"

They had dated in college but then gone their separate ways. She left for medical school and he completed a stint in Vietnam before continuing on to law school. They had met again at a New Year's Eve party in Chicago after each had married and begun their professional careers. Keith and David had become best friends and, for years, Keith had served as their family lawyer. Keith's late wife, Linda, meanwhile, had worked alongside Katherine as a pediatric nurse.

She sidled even closer and leaned her head on his shoulder. "I'm glad you were in the band. I would have hated to see you get hurt."

"Me too," he confessed. "So, do you think we should decorate for Christmas?"

"I think we have to," she replied. "Even if we won't be here right at Christmas, it's still a while until we leave for Iowa. I just didn't feel festive last year. I think David would have understood why I didn't do it but I also think he would have been a bit disappointed."

"I guess the only question is, do we use stuff we already have or get new stuff?"

"I think we do both. Let's use decorations I have here and we'll go back to your house and bring some things that you and Linda had together. Then we'll shop for some new things of our own. I'm saving Mama's things to decorate Grandma and Grandpa's house with."

"You've never actually seen it decorated at Christmas then?"

"I don't remember it at all in winter. I wish we had gone there at least once for Christmas but we lived in Virginia. Daddy was a cardiologist and Mama was a surgical nurse. They always covered other people's shifts during the holidays so *they* could travel to see their own kids and grandkids, so we were stuck at home. Besides, with the weather always so unpredictable in Virginia and Iowa and all points in between, it just didn't work for them. Daddy didn't care to fly and we came home on the train to visit in the summer.

\*\*\*\*

Alan jumped up from the couch. "Yes! Go Vikings! What an interception! Way to play defense!"

Theresa joined in from the kitchen where she and Elaine were putting away leftovers and loading the dishwasher. "Who got it?"

"Harrison Smith," he shouted back. What a catch! I can't believe Trubisky even threw that!"

The final seconds of the game had barely ticked off the clock when Theresa came down the stairs from the attic with the first of the green and red storage tubs. Alan groaned, "Already? The ham and green bean casserole haven't even settled yet."

"Yes, already," she nearly shouted. The post-game interviews gave way to Bing Crosby crooning *White Christmas* on the Bose. "Are you going to sit there or help?" she snapped.

He knew that resistance was futile. Christmas was her favorite holiday. For her, the season always began when plastic trees and six-foot Santa statues first appeared at Walmart. For him, it didn't begin until after Thanksgiving was over.

He had brought in the eight-foot, fresh-cut fir tree a couple of days ago but had convinced her to reluctantly wait on the lights and ornaments until this afternoon. He counted his blessings that Theresa did not believe in the Black Friday madness. It always irritated him that, with so much hunger in the world, people would push, shove, crowd, and even assault each other just to get a bargain on the newest 'toys'.

Alan looked out across the windswept, barren fields to the little house barely visible on the horizon and wondered what his grandparents and his great-grandparents would have thought of it all. He had to admit, although only to himself, that he enjoyed the aroma of fresh evergreen and the prospect of eggnog, frosted sugar cookies, and homemade Chex party mix. With a half-hearted agreement, he lifted himself from the recliner and dutifully followed her upstairs for the next load.

When all of the tubs were assembled in the living room, he resumed the obligatory complaining. This time, Tommy joined in, and they both received the same death stare from Theresa and Elaine. At least Elaine was now old enough to help her mother with the decorating. Working together, they filled every flat surface with colored glass balls in jars, cheesy polar bear cookie jars, and antique-looking Santa figurines of all sorts and sizes. He actually enjoyed Christmas and she knew it, but his grumping about participating in the decorating was now an annual tradition. One shouldn't mess with tradition after all. He drew the line at putting a big red plastic nose on the trophy deer head in the den. That was his 'private escape space' and he guarded it jealously.

"Okay, Scrooge," she warned, "here's the deal. You can either get the stepladder now and put the lights up on the tree or you can go to town and refresh your parents' house for their visit. Then you can come back and put them up."

"Hmph! Humbug!" he teased. "I have an idea. I think I'll go get the stepladder and put the tree lights up."

"Wise choice!"

****

Jerry was a lifelong Bears fan. Even with wintering in Florida, he carried a disdain for the Dolphins. Despite the Tampa Bay Buccaneers having been around for decades, he considered them "newbies". Both the Vikings and the Packers he considered unworthy opponents, put into the same division as the Bears only to "fill out the field". He often wondered where he had gone wrong with his son. Somewhere along the way, Alan, had turned into a rabid Vikings fan. "Crap!" he shouted at no one in particular as Harrison Smith picked off a fourth quarter pass ending what might have a game-winning drive. He was equally upset with his own quarterback for even attempting the throw. "Geez, what were you thinking? Geez!"

They still decorated for Christmas, but nowhere near as much as they had back in Iowa and practically not at all compared to what they knew Alan and Theresa would be doing today. At his moment, he didn't envy his son. As the game entered its final moments, Janice disappeared. He could hear her rummaging through the closet down the hall. She returned with a single plastic tub containing the sum total of all of the ornaments they owned since moving. They enjoyed Christmas and had often considered doing more. When Christmas came around each year, though, it just didn't seem right with the blue water and the sunny beach just yards away. "I wonder how they get in the mood in Australia," he asked, "where it's the middle of the summer."

She waited for it. She knew it was coming. It did every year. Once he said it, at least it could be put behind them for another year. "Do you suppose they sing kangaroo carols?"

He pulled up a stool to the kitchen island and opened the laptop to look again at the pictures that his cousin, Kate, had forwarded earlier. He was the only one in the family who called her Kate. It had been that way ever since their childhood when she visited the farm,. To everyone else, she was *Katherine*. "Janice, look what she's done with the living room. It looks just like it did when I was a kid! Grandma told me she had wanted to find furniture like she saw in the Montgomery Ward Catalog back in the thirties when she and Grandpa didn't have either the room or the money. Instead, she said Mom and Aunt Lilly talked her into getting a matching set of the mission-style stuff. I felt that she regretted giving in. Her friends still had their overstuffed chairs and sofas with crocheted doilies to protect the arms and backs. She said the wooden armrests never felt right. She did insist on the faux-Persian area rugs though. Grandpa refused to get rid of his old platform rocker and I think she envied how comfortable he looked in it.

I love the library table in front of the window. I used to sit at the one just like it and draw pictures or write stories on the back of torn-off calendar pages. Grandma and I would sit there when Mom and Dad were away and she and Grandpa were babysitting me. She helped me with my homework. I had no idea how much I would miss that those times."

"I think it's that way with a lot of things." Janice answered. "We don't appreciate them until later. I miss when I was a little girl and we didn't have a TV yet. I know there was a lot of unpleasant crap going on in the world but Julie and I didn't really know about it. Of course, we were too young to pay much attention and Mom and Dad didn't talk about it much either. In the winter, we played a lot in our room with our dolls and in summer we made tents in the back yard by throwing sheets over the clothesline. That was pretty much our world."

"Geez, Janice! Look at us. We're two old people sitting here making each other homesick. I wonder if the bowling alley is open on Thanksgiving."

"Probably," she answered. "Everything else seems to be these days."

# CHAPTER IX

Mildred stared out the window at the barn. It was snowing again – not the wispy, powdery stuff that blows across the field and leaves the corn stubble bare. No, it the heavy, wet snow that Harry always hated when he was tending the stock. It was the kind that piles up on the window sills and the dividers that surround the panes. It was the kind that clusters on the farm equipment left to sit out over the winter, making it appear as some mythical creature from a child's fairytale book. It was the kind of snow that sticks to hats, gloves, coats, and scarves, leaving them wet and steaming when warmed up by the fire. Strange though, she didn't feel the cold draft that always seemed to find its way into the kitchen this time of year even after the new furnace was put in. She glanced at the calendar. She didn't recall tearing off the November page. Yet it was gone. December 25 was circled in red but she had no idea what day it was now. She thought she heard the familiar pop, pop, pop of Harry's John Deere "B" but saw nothing. In a daze, she wandered to the living room and planted herself in the platform rocker. A small boy sat at the table by the window and turned around to face her. The encounter was fleeting. "Jerry?"

"Grandma?"

****

Alan turned his face away from the wind and rolled open the large metal door to the tractor shed. The array of vehicles and machines that still amazed his father would have been unrecognizable to his grandfather. There was a utility tractor that could handle jobs such as moving loads of gravel, now considered a small machine. Those same jobs would have taken his grandfather or his great grandfather an entire day or more of back-breaking labor to complete. There was the massive combine that could harvest in half a day the same amount of corn that would have taken them well over a week walking alongside a wagon and hand-wrenching each individual ear from its stalk.

There was one piece that Harry and Phillip would have found instantly familiar. In a corner of the shed sat Great-grandfather Harry's 1946 John Deere "B". It was the first tractor Harry had ever owned – purchased brand new in the same year it was released. Alan had lovingly restored it during his younger days as a 4-H project. He didn't drive it now but, in recent years, had fired it up often enough to keep it in perfect running order. His son had frequently driven it around the farm since last spring. This Christmas, however, it would become the boy's first tractor of his own.

As he climbed into the cab of the massive new John Deere 9RX, he could not help thinking again of that little "B" model. He remembered Dad talking of how they'd used it to haul round, fifty-pound bales from the field on a lowboy trailer. That was the easy part, Dad had told him. The hay which couldn't fit in the barn was stacked outside. By the time it was ready to feed out to the cattle, rain and snow had fallen between the bales, causing them to freeze together. They had to be pried loose from the stack with a crowbar. And, of course, the little tractor did not have a heated or air-conditioned cab, only a hard, cold steel seat. The only concession to winter was what they called a "Heat-Houser", a canvas covering that fit over the tractor's engine to channel some of its heat back to the driver. It was crude but it was a great improvement over driving a hay wagon behind a team of horses. Busy with his thoughts, he fired up his massive machine, stopped at the hay yard, picked up the first of the large bales, and drove past the old barn.

Theresa finished the last-minute cleaning. It was still a week and a half until Christmas but her in-laws would be arriving this afternoon from Florida and she wanted everything to be perfect. She knew Janice wasn't a white-glove housekeeper. Still, she felt funny about entertaining her in-laws in what had once been their own house. "I wonder if Janice ever felt the same way when *her* mother-in-law came over. I guess it's expected when you're the third-generation Heath wife in the same house. Oh, well. She would have preferred that Jerry and Janice stay at their own 'summer house' in town but they had decided a week ago that it wasn't worth "opening it up" for such a short visit. At least the dinner preparations were nearly complete and Elaine loved setting up the table with the Christmas china. Tommy, meanwhile, had gone out to feed the chickens.

Soon, Alan's great-aunt Katherine and her new husband would be arriving. She loved Katherine, she always had, but she was happy that the couple would be staying at the newly restored family home. Besides, she was anxious to finally see the inside of the house for herself.

**** 

Keith surveyed the mass of suitcases and other assorted luggage stacked by the front door of the condo. "Remind me again, Sweetie. How long are we going to be in Iowa?"

Katherine gave him a half-hearted glare. "Until we come back, my dear."

He knew that she had always given as well as she got. It was one of the many things that attracted him to her. "Good dodge. Maybe you should have been a lawyer instead of a doctor! Nah, probably not. Might have been awkward if we had ended up on opposite sides in court. We might have driven any sane judge nuts by the time the case was over."

"Do you really think it would have taken us that long?"

She headed back to the spare bedroom and returned with a large box that looked to be more packing tape than cardboard. "Mama' s things," she explained to his questioning look. "I'm really torn whether to bring them back when we come or just leave them there. Do you want me to show them to you now or wait?"

"I think I'd rather wait. Not much sense in unpacking them and then having to pack them right back up, is there?"

"Probably not. You've seen some of her things that I keep out." She had the contents of the box memorized, as well as those of the next box. She thought back to her own bedroom. "I still can't decide whether to take her favorite doll and the doll cradle. Speaking of her doll cradle, George and Uncle Phillip made it. I haven't ever told you about George, have I?"

"I don't think so," he answered. "Who is George?"

"It's a long story. Kind of sweet. I'll wait and entertain you with it while we're driving."

He looked again at the pile of luggage and the two boxes she had just added. "About that. I'm glad we're driving your Escalade. With my car we would have had to rent a U-Haul."

Another dirty look was shot his way and he smiled. "I suppose so. Good thing we didn't buy them bulky presents."

"Good things come in small packages," he quipped, trying to get back into her good graces. "Just like you."

"You're a piece, Keith."

The snow was worse than they anticipated. They had reservations to stay at the Westin in Moline but were now doubting they would make it that far before they had to stop for the night. "So, this is what I know about George," she began. "All of it is what I heard from Mama, Uncle Phillip, and Grandma and Grandpa. I never got to meet him when I was little since we were only there a couple of weeks each summer. As teacher, George had his summers off and always spent them working at a youth camp somewhere up in Michigan, so he wasn't around when I was. I met him briefly at Grandpa Harry's funeral service. After Grandma Mildred passed away and we quit going back, I never saw him again.

"It was a few weeks before Christmas in 1935 when he showed up at the farm," she continued. "It was snowing just like it is now ..."

"What a story!" he remarked when she had finished. "It makes me wish I had met him too. He sounds like a real gentleman."

"He was, from what Mom told me about him. The job he got was right there in Burkeville so Mom got to see him a lot when she was growing up. The whole town loved him He taught manual arts but also music. She said he was her music teacher in high school and taught there until he retired. I think he met his wife when they both worked at the youth camp but I don't recall her saying that they had children. They were both a bit older by then so I doubt they did. After he retired, I hear he kept on giving private music lessons right up until he died."

The wet snow made it more difficult for the windshield wipers to do their job. Keith could barely even make out the edge of the road. The lines were gone, completely hidden under drifts and progress was down to a crawl. He squinted as he read part of a sign where the snow had not yet stuck: "MOLINE – 70 MILES" She poured him hot coffee from the thermos but he declined, instead keeping both hands on the wheel as he tried to navigate the slippery pavement. "I'm glad you thought to buy a vehicle with four-wheel drive," he remarked. "We sure don't want to end up like those poor suckers." The cars in the median became more frequent. He hoped they were abandoned and that their occupants had already been picked up by the Illinois Highway Patrol or Motorist Assist. It was impossible to tell through the haze of snow. "Wouldn't surprise me if they shut down this section of road soon." They watched a truck with a plow churning up snow in the eastbound lanes.

"Maybe we should get off at the next exit," she told him. "I'm getting a bad feeling."

"Me, too. Hopefully, there'll at least be a truck stop  There might not be motels or they might be full already.

She having grown up in Virginia and he in Illinois, both had plenty of experience driving through the snow. It had also taught them to respect the weather. "Remind me again why we didn't hole up in Chicago for another day or two."

"I would, but I don't remember the reason myself."

"I wonder what would our grandparents have done in weather like this?" he speculated. "I think mine would have taken the train."

"I know what mine would have done," she answered. "What they always did in the winter when they could. They would have hunkered down in the house with plenty of firewood stacked in the wash-up room. They would have only ventured outside to do the necessary morning and evening chores. Grandpa told me that it got so bad once he had to take some long ropes and tie them end to end from the house to the barn so he could find his way back and forth."

A group of yellowish lights showed dimly through the snow ahead. As they drew closer, they were relieved to make out a sign CONOCO TRAVEL PLAZA. "Are you thinking what I'm thinking?" he asked her.

"Oh, yeah! I'm getting hungry too."

# CHAPTER X

In an instant, he was gone. Mildred was sure she had both seen and heard her little grandson, Jerry. But the chair at the library table was empty and the table's top was bare. There was no sign of the paper and pencil she thought he had been holding – nothing at all but a feeling to tell her that he had even been there. And yet …

On the end table was a copy of *Ladies' Home Journal*. She picked it up and noticed the date. It was the latest one, December 1955. Underneath it was a copy of *Successful Farming*, one of Harry's favorite reads, aside from his Bible and Zane Grey westerns. She leafed through the pages, perusing the latest fashions and home goods – all totally unimaginable in the Depression years when her children were growing up. After a while, she laid the magazine exactly where she had found it and got up.

She climbed the steep, narrow stairway and walked into Lilly's room. It looked just as it did when her daughter was a child. It had hardly changed from the time Lilly was small until she had married Ed and moved away. Even when they came back with their little girl, Katherine, it still looked the same. What she noticed missing were Lilly's favorite doll and its cradle that she had taken with her to her new home. Also gone was the book *The Little House on the Prairie* that Lilly had always kept on her dresser. The old over-stuffed chair where Lilly had loved to curl up and read looked newer and less worn than she remembered. She somehow knew it was no longer 1955 but wished it could be, with Phillip and Lilly there and little Katherine and Jerry running around and playing. She even briefly missed the Depression days when Phillip and Lilly were, themselves, children.

****

Theresa wondered if the dinner she was preparing would go to waste. Should she even put it in the oven or should she put everything back in the refrigerator? Her in-laws could leave Florida no problem. Whether they could land in Cedar Rapids or be diverted to some other location, or possibly even re-routed back to Florida, was another matter entirely. And even if they managed to land in Cedar Rapids, they would have to rent a car and somehow make it to the farm. She had tried to trace their flight on her computer but the Internet service had become intermittent at best. Her calls to their cell phone had gotten through but, at this point, they knew no more than she did. She sighed. Oh well, there was nothing to be done. At worst case, there would be plenty of food for her, Alan, and the kids. She wondered if Katherine and Keith had left Chicago yet or if they would delay starting out. She tried calling but either they were out of normal cell service range or their phones were turned off. She wasn't normally the nervous type but was becoming rattled. She needed a break so she made herself a cup of hot chocolate and settled into her favorite chair by the fireplace. Moments later, she heard Alan kicking the snow off of his boots in the mudroom. "Gee, Lizzy! Is it spring yet?"

"Not even close, pal," she shouted to him. "Haven't even seen any seed catalogs in the mail. Have you?"

"Nope." He poured a cup of coffee and planted himself on the sofa nearby. "I must be getting old," he announced.

"Alan, you're forty-one! I'm two years younger. Do you think I'm old, too?"

"No, my dear."

"Then what makes you think you're old?"

"I didn't say I'm *old*," he retorted. "I said I must be *getting* old. There's a difference."

"Okay. What makes you think you're *getting* old?"

"Well, for one thing, I'm really starting to understand why Mom and Dad started spending their winters in Florida, eating oranges right off the tree instead of layering-up whenever they go outside. I remember when I used to love going outside in the winter. I'd get off the school bus and race back outside to play in the snow or build a snowman or go sledding. Saturdays, especially, were made for snow."

"Well, I guess you must be getting old then," she teased. "I still like ice-skating on the pond when the snow's not on it. How about I go to the attic and fetch one of your grandfather Phillip's old canes? You need some Geritol while I'm at it?"

"You're a cold one, Theresa, but you know what?"

"No. What?"

"I still have a teenage crush on you."

She held up her empty cup. "Then use that crush for something useful, you old goat. How about you give me one of those teenage kisses and then get me some more hot chocolate? A sugar cookie would be okay too if you just happen to find one on the plate next to the toaster."

"Eew, gross!" Tommy walked in from the mudroom. "Elaine, you need to see this. Nah, maybe not. You two need to get a room!"

"We *have* a room, young man!" Theresa scolded him. "Speaking of which, maybe you should go to yours. Where did you learn such talk, anyhow?"

67

"Think I will," he mumbled back. "It's getting mushy in here."

"Me too," Elaine chimed in as she reached the bottom of the stairs then turned around. "Ugh"

"See what you started?" she laughed.

"Me? You're the one who couldn't resist the old guy!"

****

The rented Chevy Traverse arrived first. Theresa set out only a light lunch. She didn't want anyone to go hungry or to seem inhospitable. She also didn't want her guests to be too full to eat last night's dinner, which had gone unserved and now sat patiently in refrigerators in the kitchen and the garage. Janice was the first to get out and quickly received an embrace from her son. Jerry emerged and immediately headed to the tailgate to unload their luggage. "I'd forgotten how much I don't like winter!"

"Was the Traverse under cover at the rental place, Dad?" Alan asked.

"Well, yeah."

"So, you've been in the snow for, like twelve seconds?"

"Okay. But it's the longest I've been in it for two years!"

Theresa gave Alan *the look*. "So that's where you got it from?

"Got what?" Jerry inquired.

"Nothing Papa. It's an inside joke. Tommy, Elaine, give Grandma and Grandpa a hug and then let's all help bring their things inside."

It was nearly dark when the Escalade pulled into the driveway. Katherine quickly accepted Theresa's offer to stay the night. They all gathered around the dining room table. Alan offered the blessing. "We thank you, Lord, for bringing us all safely to this place . . ." After everyone was seated once more, he arose again with his glass of wine. There was, of course, grape juice for Tommy and Elaine. "I would like to propose a toast – first to our newest family member, Keith. May he still like us once he gets to know us. Second, to Grandma and Grandpa's restored house. May we all get to see the inside of it someday soon. And third, to the first of what we hope can become an *annual* tradition, a Heath family Christmas reunion. Jerry had warmed up to the idea of returning to visit every Christmas. He even admitted to Alan and Theresa that the snow was pretty – from indoors of course.

There was little talk during dinner but the lull ended as the table was cleared to make way for dessert. "Your grandma would have liked your toast," Jerry told Alan.

"But not the wine. She wouldn't have approved of the wine."

"That's for sure. They had their share of hardships. Prohibition certainly wasn't one of them. So, Keith, Cousin Kate tells us you're a lawyer."

"*Was* a lawyer," Keith corrected him. "I was a lot of things once. Scoot, I was even young once."

"How did you and Kate meet?"

Janice gave her husband a sharp jab to the ribs. "For Heaven's sake, Jerry! Let the poor man eat his dessert!"

"Katherine," Alan changed the topic, "do you want me to take you to town tomorrow? The athletic boosters always

69

have a Christmas tree lot where the tractor dealership used to be, just off the square."

"I appreciate your offer, Alan, but I've really been looking forward to cutting one here at the farm. That's what Grandpa always did. Mama told me that he always took her along as soon as she was big enough. Besides, Keith has never fetched a fresh tree before."

"Dad," Tommy asked, "can I take that old box sleigh that's in Grandpa's barn, hook it to the "B" and take them out in it."

Alan looked to Keith and Katherine for their approval.

"That old sleigh is still there?" Katherine asked incredulously. "I remember it being in the barn when we came for our summer visits. I used to play on the seat and pretend I was driving it in the snow with a pair of Grandpa's horses. But, of course, the horses were long gone by theMama used to talk about how they would ride to church in it every winter. I had no idea it was still here."

"Oh, yeah. It's here alright. I've had to do a lot of repairs on it over the years. I've replaced so much of it, I'm not sure I could tell you now how much of it's even original. Anyway, we usually take it out this time of year for school kids to come out and have a hayride in it and then a hot dog roast."

How wonderful! When?"

"We did it last week."

Jerry chimed in. "I remember Dad telling me about Grandpa's favorite horses but I don't recall their names."

"Gretchen and Gertrude." Katherine said. "They were Gretchen and Gertrude. I still have a picture that Mama drew of them when she was little. It's in my dresser drawer in the condo. I should have brought it along and put it in her room. Maybe next time."

"That's a funny coincidence," Jerry chimed in. "I still have one that I drew of Grandpa Harry's John Deere."

"So, Dad?"

Alan decided to go ahead and spoil the surprise. "I don't see why not. It's your tractor!"

"You really mean it? Tommy exclaimed. It's really mine now? Wow! That's just what I was wanting for Christmas but I figured you'd say I wasn't old enough yet. Geez, Louise! You aren't teasing, are you?"

"Well, no! I like to tease but that would be mean!"

"Geeze, Louise!"

****

Mildred again heard the familiar "pop, pop, pop" of Harry's "B". She looked out the kitchen window. The day before yesterday the snow had made it difficult to make out more than a few yards in front of her. Finally, yesterday morning, the snow had stopped, but the sky was still a depressing dull gray accompanied by a blustery north wind. This morning, the wind had subsided and the sky was a bright, cloudless blue. At the horizon, the blue faded to white. If not for the line of trees, it would have been impossible to tell where the sky stopped and the earth began.

This time, the tractor appeared along with the box sleigh. She saw three figures. One was driving the tractor and two were bundled against the cold together in the sled. The two in the sled were laughing and talking. She watched the sleigh cross the road into the south pasture and disappear over a small knoll.

****

Tommy was glad he had remembered to wear sunglasses. The glare of the sun on the snow would have been blinding. He sat proudly for the first time on the seat of his very own tractor. Tall for his age, like his father and grandfather had been, he had long been able to reach the pedals. Beginning last spring, he had driven the tractor all over the farm on small errands. But this was different. Now the tractor was *his*. He sat proud and straight as he chauffeured Katherine and her new husband in search of the perfect tree.

In Katherine's mind, the south end of the pasture that bordered the dormant corn field was full of perfect trees. They weren't perfect like the expensive ones found in the commercial tree lots in Chicago. The trees found in the city had lived among straight rows of their clones on a tree farm, miles away. The one she wanted now hadn't been planted, pampered and groomed for its entire life into the ultimate version of itself before being harvested and loaded onto a flatbed semi-trailer. No, the 'perfect' tree for Grandma's living room had sprung years ago from a single, random pine cone dropped from its parent. It had taken root with no assistance in the dark Iowa soil and had grown up largely un-noticed. It's branches, thick and green, had matured through the seasons without grooming or trimming. It had provided shelter to generations of cardinals or finches and perhaps still contained an abandoned nest. It was the tree that Mama would choose if she were here.

They passed it twice but decided to make one more circle around the two-acre frozen pond in case they had missed one. "That's it!" Katherine shouted, pointing excitedly. "That's the one right there!" Keith was skeptical. Both his mother and his late wife had been 'elegant' decorators. Their trees had always been the cream of the crop, carefully chosen after hours of scouring endless tree lots, before being delivered and decorated by grim-faced employees – not elves, but grown men in cheesy looking elf costumes. The ornaments and all the rest of the Christmas glitter in the house had come from Macy's, Bloomingdales, or Marshall Field, in matching color themes and understated hues. Like David and Katherine, Keith and Linda had never had children. In their case, it wasn't for lack of desire. It just never happened. When it became apparent that they would never have biological children of their own, they had discussed adopting but somehow never gotten around to it There were no child-made ornaments from pre-school or elementary school and no soft, childproof bears and snowmen hanging from the lower branches. The idea of a free-range tree, as Katherine had explained to him, seemed entirely foreign. Despite his hesitations, in the short time they had been together, he had already learned the folly of arguing with her. Once it was clear that she had made up her mind, it was best to smile and throw up one's hands in mock surrender. Tommy picked up the limb saw he had tossed into the sled and began working on the tree.

Mildred watched in wonder as the little tractor and sled returned from across the road and headed up the drive toward the house. It was indeed Harry's tractor, not rusted and worn-out as he had left it but bright green and shiny, just as it looked when she had first seen it. A boy who looked just like her son, Phillip when he was eleven or so, and then later Jerry at that same age, jumped from the seat and ran back toward the sled. The older man, whom she did not recognize, exited the sled and assisted the woman. She did not recognize the woman either but something seemed strangely familiar. The boy and the man each grabbed an end of the tree and headed toward the house. They proudly laid the tree on the porch. "Come on, Katherine."

"Katherine? Is that you? It can't be. You're just a little girl. Katherine?"

She waited with anticipation but no one came in. Instead, the boy hopped back on the tractor and the couple got back in the sled. They headed toward the house a mile or so away. Her disappointment was brief. Only a short time later, a strange-looking vehicle pulled up near the house. It was large and unlike any car or truck she had ever seen. It reminded her of Harry's new Chevy station wagon but it was larger. Katherine emerged from the passenger door and the unknown gentleman pulled a large, worn cardboard box from the back seat.

"Keith, honey, let me get the door for you."

"Keith?" At least he now had a name. "Harry," Mildred shouted, heard only by her husband, "come here! We have company. You've got to see this!"

"I'm so anxious to see it for real, Keith!" Katherine exclaimed. "The pictures look like they did a wonderful job of staging it but, now, we're finally here!"

"You first, my dear."

They started with the wash-up room. "I feel giddy. It's just like when we would first get here in the summer! Look! There's the cast iron sink and the pump – the washing machine, the food freezer, the cream separator, the Hoosier cupboard. It's all here!"

The kitchen was even better. "You know what?" Katherine asked him excitedly. "You're going to think I'm crazy but I think Grandma Mildred and Grandpa Harry are here. I can feel them watching us." She smiled widely as she walked to the sink and turned on the water. "Look, red and white gingham curtains She ran her hand across the Formica countertops and opened the refrigerator with her shaky hands. "I can't believe this!"

"She looks so happy!" Mildred told Harry. "I just want to hug her."

"You can't, you know," he replied.

Katherine and Keith moved on to the living room. "I know just where I want to put the tree," she said, pointing excitedly to the far corner of the room. "And, over there! I used to sit and color at that table by the window."

"Yes, you did, child" Mildred agreed.

Keith was still holding the cardboard box. "Where do you want this?"

"Just set it on the library table for now but open it up and hand me that book on top."

He pulled out the book. *"The Little House on the Prairie,"* he announced as he handed it to her. "How appropriate!"

"Let's go upstairs. I want to see Mama's old room again.

Still clutching the book, she headed through the kitchen and bounced up the stairs.

"What about the tree?" he shouted after her.

"It can wait. Come on."

Harry and Mildred were already waiting for them at the top of the stairs, outside their own bedroom door.

Katherine opened the door and peeked in. Everything looked just as it did when she first was here and saw Lilly as a little girl - the full-size bed with its ornate headboard, the chenille bedspread, the chair in the corner - all of it. She walked over and ran her hand across the bedspread before carefully placing the book in its rightful place on the dresser. "It's perfect," she announced. "It's all perfect."

Harry and Mildred watched as Keith brought in the tree and set it up where Katherine had told him. While he carried their luggage up the stairs, Katherine began opening boxes and pulling out Christmas knickknacks and tree ornaments. First to emerge were strings of lights with blue, red, and green bulbs – not mini lights or LED's but the big ones connected by large, green intertwined cords. Next were the shiny, foil icicles and carefully preserved glass balls. Last came the carefully folded but fragile tinfoil stars. "Look, Harry. Those are the stars that Lilly made at school that Christmas you got your guitar and she got her pony!"

When they had finished decorating the tree, Katherine set about placing various other items she had brought with her around the house. Mildred stared in awe. "There's our nativity set! There's my candy dish! Lilly saved all of it and kept it for Katherine!"

"I guess that's it." Katherine looked around to satisfy herself that all was as it should be. "Let's go stock up on groceries and then I think it's time to invite the family in."

More strange-looking vehicles appeared in the driveway. The giant station wagon was back along with the rental Traverse and Alan's Ford F-250. People began climbing out, loudly slamming doors behind them and chatting excitedly among themselves.

Mildred stood next to Harry and watched the procession. "I was so hoping they would be back," she said with a wistful smile. If she could shed tears of happiness, she knew she would have. "And, now, here they are, all grown up and so happy!"

"Finally. I was beginning to wonder if we would ever get to see it," Jerry commented.

"Come on, Grandpa!"

"Is that little Jerry? Why, he's all grown up! And the youngster who called him Grandpa. He's the one I saw driving your tractor when they brought the Christmas tree! Gracious! That boy looks just like Phillip and Jerry did when they were that age! Who's the girl?" Mildred's eyes darted from person to person, excited and confused all at once. *How was this all possible?*

Everyone was silent as they walked into the house. Jerry was the first to speak after they had all crowded into the wash-up room. "Kate, this is amazing! And I can't believe Alan and I were about to tear it down! I'm so glad you talked us out of it. It looks just like it did when we were kids!

"Did you hear that, Harry?" Mildred uttered. "They were going to tear it down!"

"You haven't seen anything yet," Katherine told Jerry, "Here, let me show you the rest."

The tour went on for some time. Katherine led the group to each room, pointing out things the designer had done. Since only she and Jerry had seen it as children, they shared all of the details. "That's where I helped Grandma Mildred bake bread. That's where your grandfather and I sat for hours playing Monopoly."

Elaine stood looking at the Frigidaire refrigerator. "It's so small, Katherine. It looks funny!"

"You really think it's small and looks funny, sweetheart? Before they had electricity, my grandma had just an insulated wooden box with ice in it to keep everything cold. and they didn't even have a freezer. Tommy looked at the wooden box attached to the wall. He had seen ones like it before in pictures but never in person. "That was their telephone?" he asked in dismay.

He started to pull his cell phone from his pocket. Katherine gave him a glaring look. "Put that back, young man. Don't even think about it!"

Harry commented to Mildred, "I wonder what that was about."

"I have no idea."

Most of them lingered a while but eventually the evening chores called. Theresa announced that dinner would be at precisely seven o'clock. One by one, the strange vehicles disappeared from the driveway, but not before Katherine invited everyone over for Christmas Eve dinner.

Harry and Mildred were again alone in the house. "Well, Mildred, that was something, wasn't it?" Harry asked her.

"I'm glad they'll be coming back for dinner on Christmas Eve," she answered. "That will be so nice to watch."

\*\*\*\*

Christmas Eve started out cloudy and cold. By noon, it had started to snow. By mid-afternoon, it was coming down heavily. Katherine looked out the window at the barren trees. On another day, the scene outside might have depressed her but not today. Grandma Mildred's kitchen was bright and filled with the aromas of fresh-baked, made-from-scratch dinner rolls and pumpkin pie. Elaine offered to help and they chatted happily as Katherine prepared to put the Christmas ham in the oven.

Keith was an excellent cook himself. Today, though, he was satisfied to let the two ladies have the kitchen to themselves as he arranged the place settings on the round oak table. To accommodate everyone for dinner they would have to use the kitchen table as well but for now that was off-limits. He quietly hummed Christmas carols to himself as he carefully laid out bread plates, salad bowls, and silverware.

The rest of the family filtered into the kitchen as evening approached. Unseen and unheard, Harry and Mildred watched in wonder at the increasing bustle that their home had not seen in so many years.

Keith had finally been able to complete his assigned task of setting the kitchen table. Alan and Theresa agreed to eat there with Elaine and Tommy. Before their meal, however, all of them gathered around the large table as Jerry offered the blessing. "Before we sit down to eat," he added after he had finished, I would like to offer a toast. Alan, Theresa, Tommy, Elaine, go to the kitchen and get your glasses." Out of deference to Harry and Mildred's teetotalling ways, they had all agreed not to serve wine. "First, to Katherine and Keith for bringing this house back to life along with all of its cherished memories."

"Here! Here!"

"Second, to the first of many annual Heath family Christmas dinners in Grandma and Grandpa's house. If they were here with us, I hope they would be proud and pleased."

"We *are* here," Mildred whispered, "And we *are* proud and pleased."

"Kate," Jerry remarked, "these dishes are just like the ones Grandma always got out for Sunday dinners and holidays. How did you manage to find ones just like them?"

"Oh, that part was easy." She smiled. "These *are* Grandma's dishes. She left them to Mama and Mama left them to me."

"So, what are your plans for the house now that you've gotten it all fixed up?"

"Well, we don't plan to move here full-time," she answered "I love living in Chicago, especially now when the condo isn't lonely like it was last year. But I want to come back every once-in-a-while to see all of you and to just *be* here. I especially look forward to our annual Christmas dinners. As for the house, I want to open it up from time to time so that school groups and such can see what life was life for their grandparents and great-grandparents when *they* were young. If you'll help, I'd like to rebuild some of the out buildings like the chicken house and machinery shed – maybe even put in a garden. I think that would enhance the experience."

"I'm in," Tommy answered enthusiastically. "Maybe I can turn it into a 4-H project."

"Me, too," Elaine joined in, followed by her parents.

All eyes turned to Jerry, who simply smiled his consent. "Of course, just don't count on us in the winter except for at Christmas."

Tommy couldn't help himself. "Grandpa, you're such a wimp!"

After dinner was finished and the dishes and leftovers put away, they all gathered in the living room. Jerry excused himself briefly and returned from the car with a worn and battered leather case.

"Harry!" Mildred gasped. "That's your guitar!"

"Well, so it is," he answered. "So it is."

"Play something, Grandpa," Tommy and Elaine asked in unison.

"You've got to sing too, Dad," Alan chimed in. "We'll all join in."

Jerry fondled the guitar, running his fingers gently over its pristine surface. "I've never gotten over this feel," he announced. "I can imagine myself as Grandpa Harry when he saw it for the first time. How excited he must have been!"

"I was! And how thankful to George!" Harry added, though they didn't hear him.

Jerry began slowly and softly strumming the guitar's strings. *Away in a manger, no crib for a bed...*

"Harry," Mildred shouted without interrupting the song, "he sounds just like you!"

Harry placed his arm gently around her. "No, my dear. He's much better!"

"Hogwash, you old coot," she laughingly scolded him. "No one will ever be better!"

\*\*\*\*

Alan looked at his watch. "Well, it looks like we need to be on our way. Don't want to be late for the candlelight service."

Harry and Mildred stood at the window, and watched taillights fade into the snow. "Merry Christmas, Mildred," Harry whispered, taking her hand in his.

She squeezed his fingers in return.

"Merry Christmas, Harry. I think we best get back to Heaven now so we don't miss the Christmas party up there. What do you think?"

"I think they'll all be fine here without us. Let's go. By the way, I think I heard them say they're going to do this every year."

Made in the USA
Monee, IL
11 December 2019